CUENTO
DE LUZ

For our family, which will always be our home.
—Ariel Andrés Almada and Sonja Wimmer

STONE PAPER®
NO TREES - NO WATER - NO BLEACH

This book is printed on **Stone Paper** that is **Silver Cradle to Cradle Certified®**.

Cradle to Cradle™ is one of the most demanding ecological certification systems, awarded to products that have been conceived and designed in an ecologically intelligent way.

Certified
B
Corporation

Cuento de Luz™ became a **Certified B Corporation** in 2015. The prestigious certification is awarded to companies that use the power of business to solve social and environmental problems and meet higher standards of social and environmental performance, transparency, and accountability.

Family
Series: Family Love
Text © 2022 by Ariel Andrés Almada
Illustrations © 2022 by Sonja Wimmer
© 2022 Cuento de Luz SL
Calle Claveles, 10 | Pozuelo de Alarcón | 28223 | Madrid | Spain
www.cuentodeluz.com
Original title in Spanish: *Familia*
English translation by Jon Brokenbrow
ISBN: 978-84-18302-84-8
1st printing
Printed in PRC by Shanghai Cheng Printing Company, March 2022, print number 1852-5

Family

By Ariel Andrés Almada

Illustrated by Sonja Wimmer

I'm going to tell you a secret.
One that's as old as the stars.

A secret that parents have told their children, who then tell their own children, by the fireside.

They say that before we're born,
our soul is at peace.
That it floats through the heavens,
waiting for its moment.
That every now and again it looks
down upon Earth,
and smiles as it imagines
what its new life will be like.

They also say that in the universe,
nothing happens by chance.
That some things are written in stone,
and that others can be changed.
That destiny is a sweet, gentle melody,
and that in order for it to be even
more beautiful,
we need company.

The stars are always looking for kindred spirits,
and they send them, one by one, down to Earth.

Some come before. Some come after.
But there's always a thread that connects us at some time or other.

That's why, if you pay attention
and look into the eyes of the people
around you, you'll see that we're here to
look after you and watch over as you sleep
on nights when there is no moon.

It's true that the thread sometimes gets all tangled up.

But with patience and good will,
even the trickiest knots
can be untangled.

And so, every time you get the feeling that everything around you is filled with thorns, just turn around for a moment and take a look behind you.

There, your home will always be waiting for you, where everything can be sorted out.

And if you sometimes think
that we're all very different
and that we've chosen different
paths…

…just remember that the universe knows what it's doing and that it trusts that we'll be much stronger together.

So everything's perfect
just the way it is.
And that's why today,
together here with you,
I'd like to give thanks…

...because the stars have brought us together as a family and they've done it as if by magic.

Now you know the secret, too.
And you have to keep it safe in your heart.
One day it'll be your turn to tell it,
but not tonight.

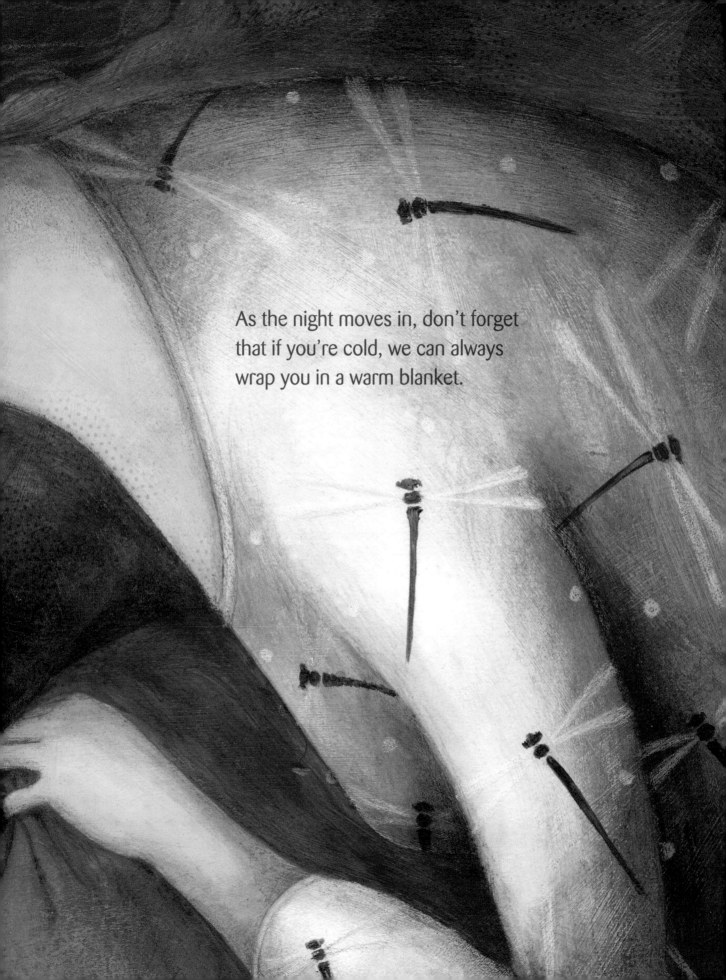

As the night moves in, don't forget that if you're cold, we can always wrap you in a warm blanket.

And your family will be here
at your side to watch over
your dreams.
And it doesn't matter if it's
winter,
spring,
summer,
or fall.